BROTHER
BORIS

LIZ PICHON

This book is dedicated to my Mark

First published in 2004 by Scholastic Children's Books
This edition first published in 2014 by Scholastic Children's Books
Euston House, 24 Eversholt Street, London NW1 1DB
a division of Scholastic Ltd
www.scholastic.co.uk

London ~ New York ~ Toronto ~ Sydney ~ Auckland
Mexico City ~ New Delhi ~ Hong Kong

ISBN 978 1407 143 255

This is me, Little Croc, and this is my family,
Mum Croc, Dad Croc and my big brother, Boris.
We all live happily in a lovely part
of the swamp.

Boris is a bit older than I am, but we still have lots of fun together. Sometimes we go swimming . . .

. . . and sometimes Boris lets me play in his room.

Our favourite game is 'Guess What I Am?'
Mum and Dad join in, but they are RUBBISH!

Boris always wins because he is the best.

IT'S TOO LOUD!

But lately Boris has been spending more and more time
with friends his own age. They all go to his room
and listen to really loud music for hours.
"TURN THAT NOISE DOWN!" shouts Dad when he's
had enough. I knock at the door. "Can I come in too?" I ask.
But nobody hears me.

Tomorrow we are having a big party for Boris
because it's his birthday. I CAN'T WAIT!
I am making a special party game for us to play.
All his friends start laughing.
"We're too old to play silly party games," they tell me.
"But Boris likes party games!" I say.
"NO I DON'T!" Boris snaps at me.
Which is not very nice, and a
bit odd because Boris and I
play games all the time.

Pin the tail on the DONKEY

When Boris isn't with his friends he looks a bit sad.
"Let's go swimming," I say to cheer him up.
"We could play 'Guess What I Am?'" I add hopefully.
"I told you . . . I'm far too old to play silly games,"
Boris says, in a really HORRID, grumpy voice.

I don't think Boris
likes me any more.

"Boris won't play with me," I tell Mum.
"All he does these days is . . .

... and hang out with his friends. Boris is just no fun any more." Mum sees that I am very upset.

So she gives me a BIG cuddle, which makes me feel much better. And we start to blow up all the balloons for the party.

The party is about to start! I am really excited, but
Boris isn't even up yet. And when he does come
out of his room, we all get a big SHOCK.

Boris is wearing
a snout ring!
Mum and Dad go
BONKERS!

They have a HUGE row, and Boris storms off back to his room.
"What about the party?" I ask.
"I don't want a stupid party now!" he shouts crossly.

I LIKE IT!
IT'S MY SNOUT!

Now I'm REALLY upset.
I go next door to see
Granny and Grandpa
Croc.

"Oh dear, looks like everyone needs cheering up,"
says Granny Croc.
"I've got a good idea," Grandpa says to me.
So we go back to the party together.

Boris is still sulking when all his friends arrive.
"We're so sorry," Mum and Dad tell them. "Boris won't come out of his room."
"But we've brought presents for him!" they say.

"And we've got a special party game," I add in a very LOUD voice.

"What a shame," says Granny Croc. "Boris will just have to miss it."

Very slowly the door begins to open . . .

... and this time it's Boris who gets a big shock!
"Can anyone guess who these lovely young crocs are?"
asks Grandpa Croc.

Everyone has a good look at the old photos.

No one seems to know, but I think I do ...

"IT'S YOU, MUM AND DAD!" I shout . . .
and I win the game.

Boris says it's the best party EVER
and all his friends agree.
Everyone sings Happy Birthday . . .

. . . and I give him his cake.

Boris even plays the party game I made.

I think I'm really lucky to have
a big brother like Boris.

Hold on, Little Croc... I'll save you!

He's the best big brother in the whole world . . .

. . . well, most of the time!

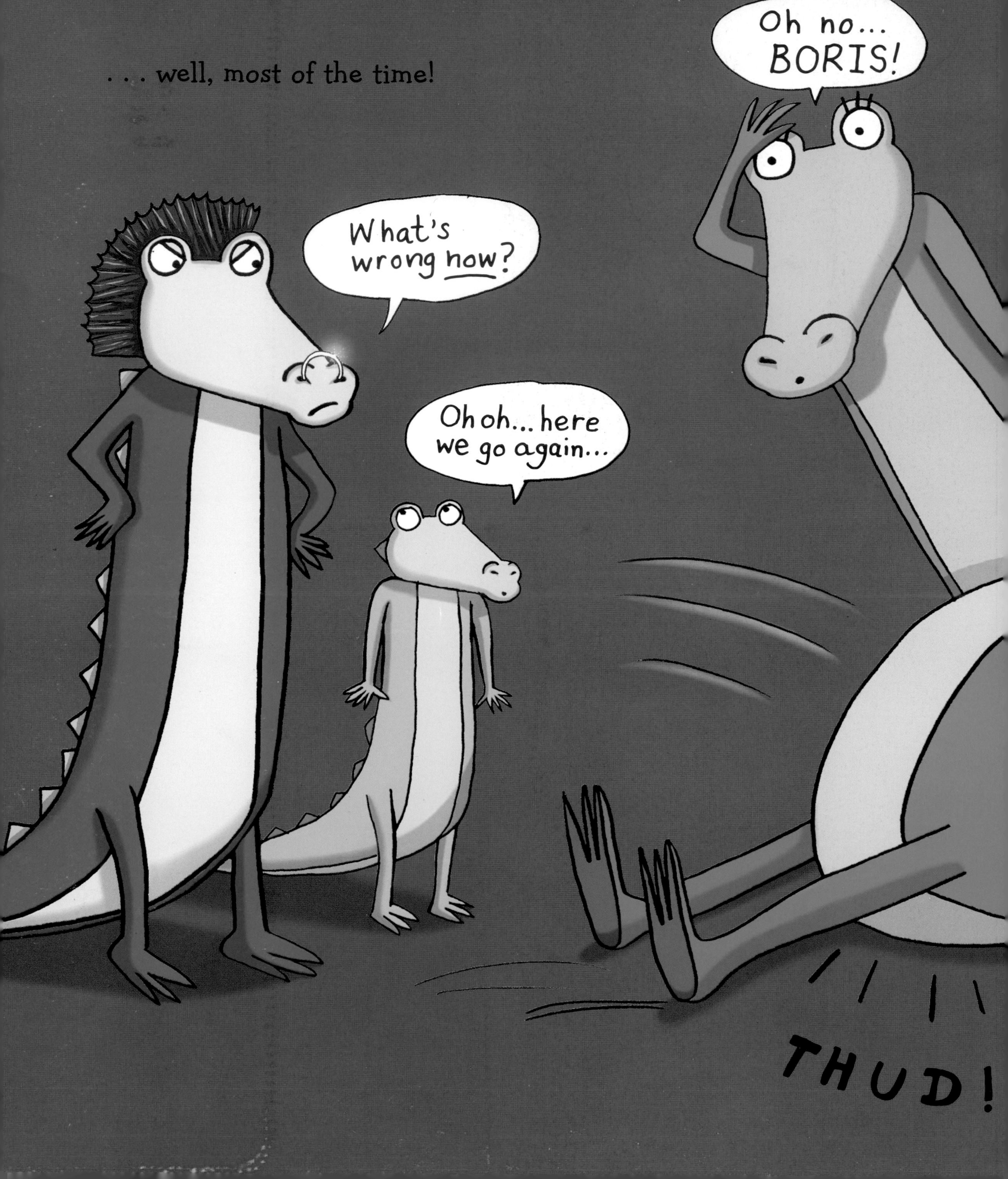